**THE TIME WARP TRIO** series

# Sam Samurai

THE TIME WARP TRIO

# Sam Samurai

## by Jon Scieszka

### illustrated by Adam McCauley

SCHOLASTIC INC.

New York  Toronto  London  Auckland  Sydney
Mexico City  New Delhi  Hong Kong  Buenos Aires

ISBN 0-439-70375-1

12 11 10 9 8 7 6 5 4 3 2       5 6 7 8 9/0

Printed in the U.S.A.       40

First Scholastic printing, October 2004

Set in Sabon

To Donna—
a real samurai *shuutome*
(mother-in-law).

Jon

# ONE

Sam stood frozen in his ready karate pose. He spoke in a low voice.

> "Do not move an inch.
> If we're where I think we are,
> We are dead meat."

"What are you talking about?" said Fred loudly. "So we're probably in Japan. I'll bet we can get some great noodles and sushi."

I wasn't sure exactly where Sam thought we were,

1

but I knew we weren't in Sam's house anymore. Fred, Sam, and I were standing on a low wooden platform that covered most of a small dirt floor room. A flickering fire burned in a rectangular pit cut into the side of the platform near the dirt floor. A metal teapot hung over the fire from a long hook in the ceiling. In the jumpy light I could just make out a few mats around the fire pit. There were no chairs, no tables, no beds.

I whispered to Sam and Fred as I looked around the room, "It sure looks like Japan, but I think we are okay because there aren't any samur—*aaiiiiieeee!*"

A crazy, wild scream exploded out of me. All three of us jumped against the wall, because there in the farthest, darkest corner of the room, looking just like the guy in the picture Sam had shown us, sat a samurai warrior in full battle gear.

Layers of shiny black and red strips of armor covered his shoulders. A breastplate and skirt kind of thing of the same strips tied with gold cords covered his chest and lower body. He wore black leather and chain arm covers, padded shin guards and foot covers, and a wild gold-horned black hel-

2

met sprouting side flaps. A thin gold sliver shaped
like a new moon topped everything off.

He sat motionless in the corner, staring at us like
we were rats in a trap.

"Oh . . . my . . . ga-ga-gosh," gasped Sam. "I
told you this is what would happen."

Even Fred, who is pretty hard to rattle, sucked
in a nervous breath.

I quickly bowed my most serious bow like I had
seen in Sam's samurai movies. "Gee Mr. Samurai
guy, we are very sorry for time warping into your

house like this. All we have to do is find our *Book* and then we'll be on our way. Okay?"

The samurai stared back at us, motionless.

"Fine? Is good? *Hola? Si?*"

The samurai stared back at us, motionless.

"Oh great," I said. "I think something's wrong with the Auto-Translator. He's not getting a word I say. Sam, you know some Japanese words. Get up here and use them."

"No way," said Sam, edging behind Fred. "I said I learned a few words. I didn't say I learned how to beg a fully armed samurai warrior not to slice off our heads with his razor-sharp sword."

Fred pushed Sam forward. "Well just say whatever you've got—hello, sorry, see ya. I don't think we want to mess with this guy."

Light glinted off the samurai's red-lipped black metal faceplate. Sam inched forward.

"Um . . . well . . . *konichiwa*, samurai. My friends and I—Joe-san, Fred-san, Sam-san—are so sorry . . . um, so *zannen* . . . for coming into your house."

A stick fell in the fire and shot up a blaze of light. The samurai seemed to look down at Sam's feet and frown. Sam looked down at his sneakers.

"Oh no." He turned to us. "Quick, take your

4

shoes off and throw them over there on the dirt part of the room."

"What?" said Fred. "He doesn't like the smell of our sneakers? This guy is starting to sound like my mom."

"No," said Sam. "It's terribly impolite to ever wear your shoes in anyone's home in Japan. He could cut our heads off for such an insult."

"He's definitely starting to sound like my mom," I said.

But it didn't seem worth it to lose our head over shoes, so we slipped them off and tossed them over onto the dirt floor. Sam bowed. Fred and I bowed along with him.

"Sooo sorry. So sorry," said Sam. "We are sorry, very sorry, I can't tell you how sorry, so please-don't-do-anything-with-your-sword-there-because-we-were-wearing-shoes-inside-your-house-and-we-are-stupid-heads sorry."

"Hey, speak for yourself," said Fred.

The fire blazed up again. The samurai in the shadows seemed to look down again.

"Oh right," said Sam. "We're supposed to kneel down in front of him because he is a samurai." Sam knelt down. Fred and I copied him.

The samurai stared at us and said nothing. Seconds drifted by. No one said anything. We looked at him. He looked at us. Seconds turned into minutes. No one said anything.

"I think he's testing us," Sam half whispered out of one side of his mouth.

"Well, I think I've had about enough testing," said Fred. "Tell him it's been real, it's been nice, but we've got a *Book* to catch."

"Patience," whispered Sam. "Samurai are impressed by patience and control."

"Maybe we can patiently back out of here," I said. "My knees are killing me."

"Please don't use that k-word," whispered Sam.

"Hey, check it out," said Fred. He nodded toward the wall closest to us. Three long spear poles with machete-style blades at the ends leaned against the wall.

"Those are closer to us than they are to him," said Fred. "There are three of us and only one of him."

Sam turned completely ghost white. "No, no, no. Don't you remember *Blade of Lightning*? Samurai are fast enough to take on ten guys with spears *and* swords."

It was too late. I could tell Fred had already made up his mind. He got up slowly, pretending to stretch his legs.

"Oh, that's it. Just needed to stretch the old—"

Then it all happened in a second. Fred jumped for the machete-spear weapon. His shadow flashed across the samurai.

"Look out Fred!" yelled Sam. "He's going for his sword!"

I dove for the samurai's feet and smacked my head on his shin guards. The samurai fell toward Fred. Fred grabbed the spear. He spun around to face the samurai, and as he turned he swung the spear with him. The samurai lunged. The blade of the spear caught the samurai just under the chin and sliced his head right off his shoulders.

The armored body part crashed to the floor. The helmeted head rolled and rolled and came to rest next to the fire pit. The red-lipped black faceplate stared at us in the light of the dying fire.

Sam and I stood up. Fred looked at the blade of the spear.

"Sorry?"

# TWO

First of all, I want you to know that Fred and Sam and I are very sorry for any trouble we might have accidentally caused in the universe by slicing off someone's head five hundred years before we were born.

Maybe one of your ancestors got turned into a monkey or a pig because of Fred's spear chop. Maybe you are a monkey or a pig because of Fred's spear chop. I don't know. We're not exactly sure what happens when someone messes with the past like we sometimes do. But we are working on it. And we are sorry. So . . . well . . . sorry, or "*eee eee*," or "*oink oink*."

Secondly, before we lose our own heads for being so impolite, for wearing shoes indoors, for moving a guy's head closer to the fire, I'd like to try to explain how we got into this latest Time Warp jam.

If you are still reading this, and haven't stomped off to go yell at the bookstore owner or teacher or librarian who would let children read such terrible things, you probably already know this is all because of a book. *The Book*. A dark blue book covered with strange silver writing and signs.

I got *The Book* as a birthday present from my Uncle Joe. He's kind of a magician. Oh, and did I mention that *The Book* can send its readers anywhere in time and space? Did I mention that the only way to return to the present is to find *The Book* in that past or future time? Did I mention that *The Book* always disappears no matter what we do and leaves us stranded when we Time Warp? Did I mention this is beginning to drive me crazy!!??

Sorry.

I guess I just get a little annoyed because Fred and Sam and I are having a hard time making this time warping thing work when even our own great-granddaughters, who are girls, and a hundred years younger than us, can figure it out and—

I'm screaming again. Sorry. This messing around with time gets very complicated. Here, why don't

I just tell you what happened. Maybe you can figure it out. If you do, send me a postcard, and we'll be happy to try your idea for hanging on to *The Book*. If you don't have any bright ideas (or are still yelling at the bookstore owner, teacher, or librarian), save your stamp.

We were over at Sam's house, working on our homework.

"Write three different examples of haiku," Sam read from the assignment sheet. "Use the form five syllables for the first line, seven syllables for the second line, and five syllables for the last line. Remember the examples we studied in class."

"Oh man," said Fred. "I can't believe it. This is such a goofball thing. Writing poetry."

Sam squinted at Fred and adjusted his glasses like he does when he's thinking. "Two more and you're done."

Fred pushed his Yomiuri Giants hat back on his head. "What?"

"You've got your first haiku," said Sam.

> "I can't believe it.
> This is such a goofball thing.
> Writing poetry."

"Wow," said Fred. "I'm a natural." He pulled out a half-ripped piece of paper and started writing it down.

"Fred, I was kidding. Hand that in to Ms. Basho, and she will freak out." Sam squinted again. "Though that's a pretty decent haiku, too.

> "Fred, I was kidding.
> Hand that in to Ms. Basho,
> And she will freak out."

"Come on, guys. Let's get serious and finish this homework. I want to show you this trick I figured out," I said. "Didn't Ms. Basho say we have to write about Japanese things like cherry blossoms or ninjas?"

"No, no, no," said Sam. "Why does every American kid think Japan is all about ninjas?"

"Because you see them in every computer game, cartoon, and kung-fu movie?" said Fred.

"Historical research shows most ninjas were just hired robbers. The real warriors in Japan were the samurai," said Sam. "Let me show you these guys."

Sam scooped up a pile of books from his mom's desk, dumped them on the kitchen table, and started flipping through them like a maniac. In case you haven't noticed, Sam's like that. He's a maniac for something different every week. Last week he knew everything about sharks. This week it was everything about Japanese samurai warriors. I don't know where he gets it. Though now that I think of it, I guess he does get a lot of that craziness from his mom. Sam lives with just his mom. She writes stuff for magazines and books and computer sites. She knows all kinds of stuff, and she's always going crazy over whatever she's working on.

13

"Look at these stone castles. Four hundred, five hundred years old. Look at these armies. Check out these swords." Sam flopped open a book to a picture of two beautiful swords, one long, one short. "The long one is called a *katana*. The short one is called a *wakizashi*. If you were a samurai, you carried both swords tucked into your sash. And here's how sharp they were."

Sam opened another book to a black-and-white drawing of samurai warriors looking at two shelves. The shelves were full of heads. Yes—heads. Just . . . heads.

"Oh man," said Fred. "I guess they were the losers."

"Definitely," said Sam. "The winning general had the heads of the losers in battle washed and combed. Then he inspected them. If the eyes were looking up, that was unlucky. Eyes looking down or closed were lucky."

"Either way sounds pretty unlucky for the guy losing his head," I said.

Sam threw out more pictures of armored and helmeted samurai in battle. "And you've got to see these movies I've been watching with my mom. She's writing this article on samurai. We've seen

14

*Seven Samurai, Shogun, Ran, Samurai—*"

"Aren't they all in Japanese?" said Fred. "I hate those movies where you have to read them."

"There's not many words in the good action scenes," said Sam. "And I started to learn some Japanese just from listening."

I looked up from the samurai warlords book. "Hey that's the trick I was going to show you. Remember when you asked how come everyone speaks English no matter where we time warp?"

"Yeah," said Sam.

"Well, you were right. I found a part in *The Book* that explains the Auto-Translator. It automatically translates everything into *The Book* user's language. Look." I pulled a thin blue book covered with silver writing and designs out of my backpack.

Sam jumped up from the kitchen table. "Are you crazy? Put that away! You know if you get that thing anywhere near those samurai books something is going to happen and the next thing you know, we'll be back in sixteen-hundred Japan with armored samurai trying to slice off our heads."

"Ah, calm down," said Fred, slapping Sam with his hat. "This sounds good. Maybe there is an Auto–Haiku Writer or an Auto–Homework Doer in there. We could put our empty papers in there. Go get a slice of pizza. Come back, and we're finished."

"I don't know," I said. "But look in the back here. I think I finally found the section that explains how *The Book* works."

That got Sam interested. "Really?" He moved one step closer. "Just don't anybody touch any pictures or read anything from *The Book* out loud."

I opened *The Book* to some strange diagrams and charts in the back. But that wasn't what got us in trouble. It was what happened next.

"So what cranks *The Book*?" said Fred.

"What triggers the time warping?" I said.

"You mean the green mist?" said Sam.

A wisp of that very mist leaked out and curled around the samurai books.

Sam jumped into his ready karate position. "Stop! No! *Yamero! Iie!*"

"What did we do?" said Fred. "What did we say?"

The whirlpool of green time-traveling mist swirled around Sam's kitchen. And just before we were flushed down four hundred years, I saw the answer. Time travel haiku.

16

"So what cranks *The Book*?
What triggers the time warping?
You mean the green mist?"

# THREE

Fred, Sam, and I stared at the helmeted head resting by the fire. It stared back at us. We were too freaked out to move.

"I guess he wasn't as fast as that guy in *Lightning Samurai*," I finally said.

Fred carefully leaned the spear back against the wall, then put his hands in his pockets. "You helped slow him down by taking out his legs, Joe. And you saved me by yelling a warning, Sam. But I didn't mean to whack his head off. I was just going to keep him covered while we found *The Book*."

"Speaking of which," said Sam. "Now I think we'd definitely better get *The Book* and get the heck out of here. I don't know all of the samurai customs, but I'm pretty sure it's not polite to remove a samurai's head."

"Shouldn't we at least clean him up or put him

back together?" I said. "Maybe no one will notice for a while."

"That is disgusting," said Sam. "How are we going to clean—" Sam looked at the armored body. Then he looked back at the head.

Soft daylight filtered into the room from outside. I heard birds chirping. The morning sun began to light the corners of the room.

Sam looked at the armor again. He looked at the head. Then he started to laugh.

"Uh-oh," said Fred. "He's losing it."

I grabbed Sam by the shoulders. "Hang on, Sam. Don't worry. We'll find *The Book*. We'll get back to your house."

Sam shook his head and only laughed harder. He tried to say something, pointing at the head. But the only sound that came out of him was something like, "Eep ooh eh urh."

Fred looked at me. "Lost it."

I nodded.

Sam broke away from me. He picked up the head and tossed it to me.

I didn't want to catch it, but I couldn't help myself. I caught the head and closed my eyes. It seemed oddly light. I opened one eye. I turned the

19

helmet and mask over. That's when I saw what
Sam had realized. It wasn't a head. It was an empty
helmet and mask.

Sam laughed. "That was no samurai. We just
beat up a suit of armor."

Fred picked up the body. The arms and legs
flopped loosely. Fred looked hugely relieved. The
morning sun poured into the room. Now we could
see we had taken on a suit of armor sitting in a
dark corner. The shadows from the flickering fire
had made it look like it was alive.

We all sat down on the edge of the wooden platform in our socks. It felt good to be alive. I held

the helmeted faceplate in my lap and looked it in the eye. "You want some more of that?"

"Yeah, come on, metalhead," said Fred. We both laughed.

"Though I do think you're right, Joe," said Sam, cleaning his glasses with his T-shirt.

"About what?"

"We should put everything back just like it was, find *The Book*, and get out of here."

For once, we all agreed. Fred sat the samurai armor back on its stool. I gave him back its head. Sam searched the room for *The Book*.

We met back at the fire pit.

"As usual," said Sam. "Nothing. Nada. No *Book*. Nowhere. Don't you guys think this is starting to get ridiculous? I mean we get thrown around time by looking at a picture, or touching some numbers, and now from saying a group haiku! And what's with the disappearing *Book*? Why can't we ever hang on to it?"

Fred frowned and pulled on his hat. That's how I could tell he was thinking. "Yeah, what's the deal with that, Joe?"

"That's what I was trying to show you," I said. "In that same section where I found out about the

Auto-Translator, there was a part about keeping track of *The Book*."

Sam's eyes lit up. "So what did it say?"

"It's called the Eternal Return," I said. "It's something about how *The Book* has to change to fit in with whatever time it's in."

"But what about holding on to it?" said Sam.

"That's the part I didn't get," I said. "It said 'Look for the books of the time,' and then it had a bunch of words in some other language and drawings and signs."

"Oh great," said Sam.

"Is that good?" said Fred.

"It's what we already know," said Sam. "*The Book* disappears, then it turns up somewhere you might find a book. Brilliant. Oh man, I just know we're going to get our heads cut off."

"That's bad," said Fred, sitting down next to Sam.

"Come on, you losers," I said, walking around the room. "Let's think. We're back in ancient Japan."

"Sixteen hundred, no doubt," said Sam.

"Did they have books then?"

"They sure don't have any tables or chairs," said Fred.

"I know they printed things with wood blocks," said Sam. "Some of their books were illustrated action books like comic books."

Fred perked up. "So maybe they hide their books like I hide my comic books so my brothers don't mess them all up."

"This is hopeless," said Sam, holding his head in his hands.

Fred scanned the room. "Like there," he said. He pointed to a small ledge on the top of a wall. "That's where I'd hide them." We looked up and saw a row of book-size packages wrapped and tied.

"I mean this is hopelessly easy," said Sam.

"Time Warp traveling mist, here we come," I said.

Fred and I boosted Sam up the wall. He stood with one foot on each of our shoulders. He stretched up and grabbed a dark blue package. That's when a shadow fell across the room.

An angry man's voice shouted a very mean-sounding string of Japanese words at us. Then we heard an even more chilling sound—the *chiiing* sound a thin sharp piece of metal being pulled from its holder might make. The sound you might imagine from a sword being pulled free for action. The last sound you might hear before your head rolled off your shoulders.

We turned slowly, with Sam still on our shoulders, toward the sound of our doom.

A man in a kimono and wide pants, a real man this time, no tricky shadows, stood in the doorway. He had two swords stuck in his belt, just like the picture of the samurai Sam had shown us. In his right hand he held the sword that had made the noise. He didn't look happy. And he was still speaking some very mad Japanese.

"What the heck is he saying?" asked Fred.

"I can't understand a word," said Sam. "But I'm guessing it's something like, 'Why are you three criminals stealing my best comic books? Stay right there. I will use my very sharp sword to cut you into tiny pieces to feed to the worms.'"

"Mr. Samurai," I said. "This is not what it looks like. We are just three innocent time warp guys looking for our *Book*. Book. Us. Ours."

The samurai guy frowned. He obviously didn't understand a word I said.

"What happened to the Auto-Translator?" said Sam.

24

"I don't know," I said. "It must have got switched off."

"Well, I hope you're good at sign language or have one very good silent trick up your sleeve," said Sam. His legs started to shake. Fred and I started to shake, too.

The samurai yelled something again. I think it was a question. But he didn't wait for an answer.

He ran up to us, drew his sword back, and prepared to strike a serious two-handed blow.

I remember looking closely at the strange little ponytail of hair the samurai had folded forward on the top of his half-shaved head. I remember seeing every detail very clearly and thinking, "We are about to get our heads sliced off by a guy with a very funny ponytail . . . but it doesn't seem that funny."

# FOUR

The samurai pointed his sword at Sam and motioned for him to get down. Fred and I slowly lowered Sam. The samurai grabbed the dark blue package roughly out of Sam's shaking hands. More pointing with his sword and Japanese shouts moved the three of us into a line.

"He's going to try to take all three of our heads off in one swipe," said Sam.

"Let's make a grab for *The Book* and open it really fast," said Fred.

"We'll never make it against a real samurai," I said.

"Joe," said Sam. "Our only hope is a magic trick—quick."

The samurai put the package down behind him, keeping his eyes on us the whole time. He drew his sword slowly back. I knew I had one chance, and probably only one chance to come up with a particularly great trick.

I thought of the magic book I was reading and what trick might impress a mad samurai. The Coin Vanish? I didn't have a coin. The Red and Black Card Switch? I didn't have cards. The Number Prediction? This guy wouldn't understand a word I said.

"*Oogala boogala*" (or something like that), said the samurai.

"Uh Joe . . . the trick?" said Sam. "Some trick. Any trick."

The lightbulb went off over my head. Sam had given me the perfect idea. Any trick. "That's it!" I said. I thought of the first chapter of every magic book I ever read. It's always about how you can make almost any trick work. You just have to command your audience's attention.

It's like when you talk to your dog or cat. They don't know what you are saying. They listen to how you say it. If you sound nice, they wag their tail or purr and rub on you. It doesn't matter if you are saying the words, "Come here doggy-woggy. I'm going to tie your ears in a knot and whack you."

I didn't need a great trick. I just needed to sound

like a great magician. I looked the samurai in the eye and said in my best stage voice, "Mr. Samurai, observe."

I had his eyes on me now.

"With nothing up my sleeve . . ." I motioned to my two bare arms, since I was wearing a T-shirt . . . "I will now present one of the most ancient and astounding tricks in the long and glorious history of magic." (I copied most of that from listening to my Uncle Joe. He's a stage magician sometimes, and he said that kind of talking while you set the trick up is called "patter.")

The samurai looked puzzled, but interested.

"I will attempt to link this ring—" I made a circle with my thumb and first finger—"with this ring." I made the same circle with my other hand and held them up.

The samurai lowered his sword down in front of him. Sam breathed a huge sigh.

I moved my hands back and forth, around and around, chanting, "Hocus pocus, toilet plunger, football touchdown, woof!"

I crashed the two circles together, then held them up, now linked together.

"*Ta da!*"

The samurai looked stunned.

I heard Sam whisper to Fred, "Now who's lost it?"

But I noticed the samurai give a half smile.

"And to reverse this amazing effect," I boomed in my biggest stage voice, "you simply reverse the spell."

I waved my linked hands around and chanted, "Football touchdown, toilet plunger, hocus pocus, woof!" I slipped my fingers apart and raised the now freed circles over my head.

"*Ta da!*"

Talk about a "Do or Die" trick.

If the samurai liked it, we lived. If not—

# FIVE

The samurai leaned back and back and . . . actually snorted a laugh.

Sam, Fred, and I started breathing again

The samurai said something that sounded like, "*Eeka waka dodo chacha* is the stupidest trick I have ever seen."

"I know," I said. "I think it's the first trick I ever learned from my dad but—hey! What did you just say?"

"Hey, I'm understanding Japanese," said Fred.

"The Auto-Translator must have kicked back on," I said.

The samurai laughed and shook his head. "That is the stupidest trick I have ever seen. Except for this one." He slid his sword back into his belt and held up two hands—one a closed fist, the other with two fingers up.

"Observe," said the samurai. "I will magically

make one finger jump from this hand with two fingers to this hand with no fingers." He waved the two-finger hand around saying, "Jump to the other hand, now!" He smacked the two-finger fist down on the other fist. He held up both hands. Each one had one finger up.

"*Ta da!*"

We laughed like maniacs.

The samurai laughed with us.

I must say he wasn't the smoothest magician I've ever seen. And he didn't have very good patter. But we were so relieved he put his sword away, he could have poked himself in the eyeball and we would have laughed.

The full morning sun blazed through the doorway. The samurai looked around the room.

"But where do you come from? What is your province? What is your family? Why did you not answer me when I first asked you?"

Sam and Fred and I looked at each other. We didn't know what to say. Finally Sam spoke up.

"We are traveling from the province very far away to the east called Brooklyn. We are looking for a lost book. It belongs to our . . . um . . . daimyo. We need to return it to him."

The samurai gave us a questioning look. "Bookalin? I don't know Bookalin. But from the east, you are surely supporters of Tokugawa Ieyasu."

"E-eyuka what?" said Fred.

"Yes, surely," said Sam.

"Who is your daimyo?" asked the samurai.

"Our leader is . . . well . . . the mayor," said Sam. "Our daimyo is Rudy Giuliani."

"Rudy Giuliani? Did he fight at Osaka?"

"Hoboken, I think," said Sam.

"Hmm," said the samurai. "No matter. It is good that you show such loyalty, and support Tokugawa. Especially in these times when so many armies are on the move. What are your names?"

"Joe and Fred, and I am Sam," said Sam, introducing us all.

"My name is Tada Honda."

"Like the motorcycle?" said Fred.

"A very old and honored name," said Sam, talking over Fred.

The samurai bowed. We bowed back.

"Sooo," I said, thinking of how to get out of there as quickly as possible. "It's been nice talking to you. But we really do have to get going. Could we just peek at your blue book there? I think we have one just like it."

Honda picked up the thin blue package. "Ah yes. One of my most precious treasures." The samurai slowly unwrapped the bundle. Fred, Sam, and I braced ourselves for the twirling thrill of time warping home. Honda opened the book and. . . and nothing happened. No time warping. No green mist. Nothing.

"It's my issue number one of Super Samurai Man," said Honda. "Look what great condition." He showed us an illustrated book of a crazy-eyed samurai guy.

"Oh," we all said, trying not to look too disappointed that it wasn't *The Book*.

"But why did you have it hidden up there?" asked Sam.

"So my little brother wouldn't find it and mess it up," said Honda.

Fred smiled.

"The only thing more precious to me is the gift given to me by my daimyo—his armor." He pointed to the suit of armor we had just put back together. "If anything happened to that, I would take the head of whoever dared touch it."

Fred quit smiling.

"Well, of course," I said. "No one should mess with a guy's armor. Everyone knows that."

"Where is your daimyo?" asked Sam. "And does he maybe have a thin blue book?"

"My daimyo was lost at the battle of Sekigahara," said Honda. "So now I am a samurai with no master. I am a *ronin*. But I have sworn to serve the master my daimyo served—Tokugawa."

Honda looked down. You could tell he still felt bad about losing his master. A single bird chirped outside. We didn't say anything.

Suddenly the sound of a ringing bell split the quiet. Honda looked up.

"A runner." He looked outside the door and down the road. "At last! It is the runner ahead of the troops of Ii Naomasa. Gather your weapons and armor. We will join the Red Devils on the road to Edo. We will go to see the great warlord Tokugawa and find the book for your daimyo Giuliani."

We sat down on the edge of the wooden platform and put on our only armor—our sneakers.

"Join the Red Devils? Travel to Edo to meet

36

Tokugawa?" said Sam. "Does that sound like a good thing? A safe thing?"

We could hear the tramping sound of horses and feet. It sounded like a lot of feet.

"Do we have a choice?" I said.

# SIX

Outside it was a beautiful spring morning. And I'm guessing the leader of the Red Devils was an amazing sight. I'm only guessing because we were on our knees, faces planted in the dirt when he passed. All I saw was an ant trying to get around a leaf.

Fred, Sam, and I had run outside right next to the road to get a good look at a real samurai army. But as soon as the first red armored bodyguard came around the corner, Honda yelled, "Down! Down!" and pushed us down into a kneeling bow. "If you want your head to stay with you, keep it touching the ground."

We heard the clomp of the horses, jingling armor, flapping flags, and tramping feet, but no voices. It was kind of spooky. After a few minutes, we were hidden in a low cloud of dust. Sam coughed and sneezed. And sneezed and sneezed and sneezed. I peeked my head up to see if Sam still had his.

Sam was rolling around on the ground, trying not to sneeze. Honda and Fred were up on one knee, still sort of bowed forward, but watching the passing procession.

And what a procession. It was not hard to figure out why they called them the Red Devils. Red-armored samurai, their two swords stuck in the left side of their belt, rode on horses done up with red harnesses, red saddles, even red stirrups. Solid red banners flapped from an L-shaped black pole stuck in a holder built into the back of the samurai's armor. There had to be at least ten or twenty horsemen all together.

"Wow," said Fred.

Next came the strangest thing. It looked like a big red and gold curtained box with two poles sticking out the front and back so guys could carry it. The curtains swayed, and you could see people inside.

"The daimyo's relatives and honored guests," whispered Honda.

Serious-faced samurai on foot carrying spears. More fancy curtained boxes being carried. Some with people, more with just bundles carried by

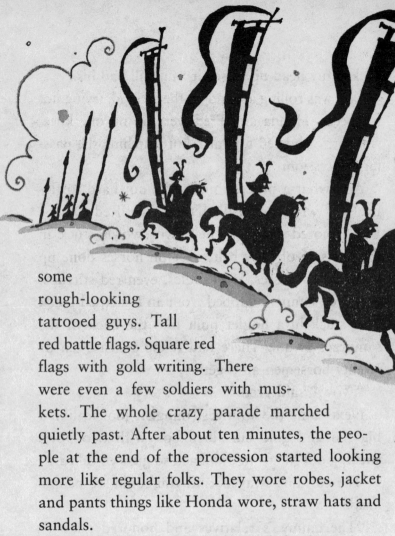

some
rough-looking
tattooed guys. Tall
red battle flags. Square red
flags with gold writing. There
were even a few soldiers with mus-
kets. The whole crazy parade marched
quietly past. After about ten minutes, the people at the end of the procession started looking
more like regular folks. They wore robes, jacket
and pants things like Honda wore, straw hats and
sandals.

Honda picked up his bundle. "When I say 'go,'
walk behind me on the road and blend in."

"Oh that's easy for you to say," said Sam. "How
are we supposed to blend in looking like this?"

I looked at the three of us wearing our usual jeans, T-shirts, and sneakers. We blended in fine in Brooklyn. In 1600 Japan we didn't look anything like anybody.

"If anyone asks, I will say you are entertainers hired by my master. I am making sure you reach him. Ready?" said Honda.

# SEVEN

As usual, we didn't get a chance to ask any questions. We just had to go.

We jumped on the road and started walking with everyone carrying boxes, bundles, and bags. No one really did seem to take much notice of us. Fred, Sam, and I followed behind Honda and walked.

We walked down a neat road of sand and stone lined with pine trees. We walked by the last of a few small houses and then we were out in the country. Rice paddies filled with water made a checkerboard along either side of the road. Women in big round straw hats stood in the ankle-deep water, planting small green rice plants in neat rows.

"Look at that," said Sam.

A beautiful, perfectly snow-tipped mountain appeared out of the clouds behind us.

"Mount Fuji," said a small, smiling bald man in a plain brown robe.

Clouds covered the mountain again.

"How pleasant—
just once not to see
Fuji through mist."

"Very nice," said Fred. "But you know what would be nicer? Something with wheels. Honda, how are you guys going to make motorcycles and cars if you're not using wheels?"

"What is 'moto-syco'?" said Honda.

"No wheels on the Tokaido Road," said the little bald guy. "Because armies moving slowly is sometimes a good thing."

"Like when the army is not a friend's," said Honda.

The bald guy laughed again. "Exactly, samurai." He looked us all over. "I don't believe I have seen you before. May I ask, what is your name?"

"Honda," said our samurai, and nothing more.

"I am known as Bakana Zou," said the man.

"Silly Elephant?" translated Honda.

"But you may call me Zou," said the smiling little man.

Everyone in front of us suddenly stopped.

"And that is also why we have so many gates and passport checks," said Zou.

"Gates?" said Fred.

"Passport checks?" said Sam.

"But of course," said Zou. "When were you born? As it has always been on the Tokaido Road, just as this notice says." Zou tapped a wooden sign at the side of the road and read it aloud:

> "Passports are required of all persons.
> Persons suffering from insanity,
> prisoners, decapitated heads (male or
> female), and corpses (male or female)
> must show passports."

Honda looked concerned. "You have no passports from your province of Bookalin?"

"Uh . . . no . . . not exactly," I said.

"Oh now we are toast," said Sam. "I told you we should have stayed."

"Can't we just sneak around through the fields?" said Fred.

"Oh no," said Honda. "Guards." He made a slicing sword motion.

"Forget it," said Sam. "We are turning around right now."

"But you know *The Book* is probably at this shogun's castle," I said. "That's always the way *The Book* works. And it's the only way we'll really get home."

The line of people moved up. Now we could see

the gate across the road. Everyone was showing a passport.

"Does everyone have to show a passport?" I asked Zou. "Aren't there any exceptions?"

"Forget it," said Sam. "If even bodyless heads need passports, we are cooked."

"Sumo," said Zou. "Sumo never need passports. Not easy to hide sumo. Are you sumo today?" Zou cracked himself up again with his own bad joke. "Or performers. If you can show a good enough trick. Are you performers today?"

Fred and Sam looked at me.

The line moved forward.

It all became painfully clear. Once again I had one chance to come up with a good trick.

The line moved forward.

And this time it looked like it was going to have to be something a little better than the Magic Finger Rings trick.

I looked ahead and saw an awful lot of swords and spears up at the passport check gate.

I remember thinking, "Something way better than the Magic Finger Rings trick."

# EIGHT

You know, now that I think of it, time warping really isn't such an unusual thing. It happens to people all the time. When you can't wait for something good to happen—like Friday afternoon and getting out of school for the weekend—that hour from 2:00 to 3:00 can take forever. When you want time to go slow—like when you have to go to the doctor's and get a shot in a week—seven days can whip by in the blink of an eye.

Time warped. I blinked. And the next thing I knew, Fred, Sam, and I were standing in front of a pinched-face man at the wooden guard gate across a bridge. He had already checked Honda's and Zou's passports. Now he had his hand out for ours.

"Papers," he ordered.

"We are entertainers," I said. "From the far-away province of Brooklyn."

The gatekeeper frowned. He looked like one of those unhappy guys who always think the worst about other people.

"You look like runaway boys in very bad clothing," said the gatekeeper, eyeballing us suspiciously.

Honda came back with one hand on his sword handle. He looked down at the gatekeeper and spoke harshly to him. "They are entertainers," said Honda. "I am escorting them."

You could almost see the gatekeeper shrink under Honda's stare. "Of course, samurai. As you say, samurai."

Fred, Sam and I couldn't believe it. Just like that we were free. I didn't have to come up with a trick, which was a good thing because I hadn't thought of anything. We walked through the gate and looked at the buildings of Edo in the distance.

The gatekeeper gave a little bow, still looking us over. He looked at us like a snake watching a frog.

"But according to law, they must show their entertainment," said the gatekeeper.

Honda turned to argue.

The gatekeeper smiled a thin, mean little smile, now looking like the snake who swallowed the frog. A group of travelers, hearing the word "entertainment," started to gather around us.

Honda didn't want to draw any more attention to us. He could only agree.

Sam fiddled nervously with his glasses. "Okay Joe, let 'em have it."

Fred pounded me on the back. "Abracadabra."

I looked at Sam. I looked at Fred. I didn't have the heart to tell them—my mind was a complete blank. It was like one of those horrible nightmares where you show up for math class in your underwear and find out there is a test you didn't know about.

Except this was a nightmare I couldn't escape by waking up.

"Well?" said the gatekeeper. I was scared stiff. I was scared speechless. I didn't know what to do.

And then the strangest thing happened. I still don't know if it really happened, or if my stalled brain just made it up.

I looked at the crowd waiting for the trick. The smiling face of Zou caught my eye. He nodded toward the doorway of the gatehouse. I looked just in time to see a bird spreading its wings and flying out of the doorway. I looked back at Zou. He nodded and flapped his arms once like wings.

Now you may think I'm crazy. In fact, I think I'm crazy, because everything suddenly came together in my mind and hit me like a lightning bolt. All from Zou and a bird and a doorway. But how did Zou know I would know? Did I really see a bird? Did Zou really flap his arms?

I didn't have time to answer any questions. I had to get to work showing my Mental Powers in the Flapping Arms trick.

"Of course," I said, scanning the crowd for a friendly face. This trick works best on somebody who wants to believe you. "We don't normally unleash our full Mental Powers because they can be so . . . frightening," I said. I found a kindly looking older lady smiling and nodding. "But I can show you a small glimpse of my Mental Powers by giving this lady the mind of a hawk, freed from its cage, spreading her wings to fly."

The gathering crowd laughed and clapped their hands. Zou nodded, smiling. The gatekeeper frowned. I led the lady over to the doorway. I stood her inside it with her feet in each corner.

"Close your eyes," I said in a low even voice. "Do not speak. You are a hawk trapped in a narrow cage." I moved her arms so the back of her hands touched against the inside of the doorway. "Push your wings up and against the cage."

The lady closed her eyes and pressed her arms up. The crowd leaned forward to spot any tricks.

"Keep pressing your wings against the cage. You want to be free," I said.

The other secret of the trick is to keep your patter going for at least a solid minute. I filled it with a lot of talk about the cage closing in, the hawk wanting to be free, wanting to lift her wings and fly away.

I looked around the circle of spectators. Travelers, and now some soldiers, watched the lady carefully. Fred, Sam, and Honda were sucked in too.

The beautiful part of the trick is that it isn't really a trick or Mind Power at all. It's more like

a reflex. After your muscles press for so long, they automatically tighten when you stop pressing.

I kept up my patter. The tension built. "When I count to three," I said, "I will release you from your cage. Then you can step forward, drop your arms, and your wings will rise. One. Two. Three."

The lady opened her eyes and stepped forward. I held my breath. Her arms hung loose and then to her surprise, they rose, rose, rose up to her shoulders. The crowd oohed and ahhed.

The lady laughed and covered her mouth. "I felt my wings! I wanted to fly!"

The crowd clapped and cheered. Even the lemon-sucking gatekeeper looked amazed.

"Joe the Magnificent," yelled Fred, raising a fist in the air.

I bowed.

And life would have been great—if a certain red-armored samurai hadn't chosen that moment to ride up on his horse.

"What is all this noise?" the samurai demanded. He had a scar that made his lip curl into a nasty sneer. Even his horse looked mean, stamping around. The crowd backed away, leaving Fred, Sam, and me.

We copied everyone else bowing. Zou stepped forward to save us. "A small entertainment, sir."

The samurai scowled down at us. "No one disturbs our master's peace with their entertainments unless they ask me, leader of the Red Devil bodyguards, Owattabutt." The samurai posed proudly.

Fred's eyes bugged out. I couldn't stop him.

"Oh what a butt?" asked Fred.

"Owattabutt of Minowa," said the samurai.

"Oh—what a butt," repeated Sam.

We tried our best not to laugh. We really did. But you know us.

It took us about three seconds to crack up, freak out Owattabutt, have our hands tied behind our backs, and get surrounded by a gang of red samurai warriors with spears.

Then things really went bad.

Owattabutt gave us a very nasty look and said, "Now you will *woof woof woof bark bark bark meow meow meow.*"

# NINE

"Let me guess," said Sam, staring at the point of the closest spear. "Something's wrong with the Auto Translator again."

"*Eeka weeka wakka*," said Owattabutt.

"I think so," I said. "But I don't know how . . . if we don't even have *The Book*."

"*WAKKA WEEKA EEKA!*" screamed Owattabut. He was standing right over us now. The samurai spears closed in.

"Sam, what's he saying?" said Fred.

"I'm guessing it's something like, *'Let's poke Fred full of holes for laughing at my name!'*" said Sam.

"You laughed, too," said Fred.

"Only because you started," said Sam.

"I don't think so," said Fred.

"I think so," said Sam.

Owattabut spoke loudly and slowly, one word at a time.

"*Ichi.*"

"What is that?" I said.

"*Ni.*"

"It sounds familiar," said Sam.

"*San.*"

"Well don't hurry," I said. "But just let us know what it is before we get poked full of holes, okay?"

"*Yon.*"

"Sam?" I said.

"*Go.*"

"Go?" said Sam. "That's 'five.'"

"*Roku.*"

"Six," said Sam.

"*Shichi.*"

"Seven," said Sam. "He's counting."

"*Hachi.*"

"Eight," said Sam.

"He's counting?" I said. We all realized what was happening at the same time, but there was no time to time-warp slow it down or stop it.

"*Kyu.*"

"Nine," said Sam in a very squeaky voice.

"He's counting to ten before he gives the order to do us in!" I yelled.

Fred, Sam, and I backed against each other, but there was nowhere to go. Hands tied behind our backs, circled by samurai spears, we had just one more number.

And we didn't need a translator to tell us it was a final "ten."

# TEN

"**S**top!" yelled a girlish voice.

"Stop?" said Sam. "I thought '*ju*' was ten."

"Hold your spears, samurai. These boys are special friends to the Lady Ii Naomasa," said the voice.

I opened my eyes, which I hadn't even realized I had closed.

Owattabutt looked like he was going to explode. His face was almost as red as his armor.

The girl who had spoken waved to us from the bridge. She wore a bright green kimono. Two other girls stood with her.

Fred, Sam, and I had no idea who they were, but we waved back.

Owattabutt spoke to the girls. "I have disappointed Lady Ii Naomasa. I request permission to kill myself."

"Permission denied," said a lady, stepping out

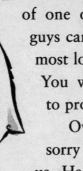

of one of the traveling boxes the guys carried on poles. "You are the most loyal warrior of the regiment. You were performing your duty to protect Lord Ii as you should."

Owattabutt bowed deeply. "So sorry for my rudeness," he said to us. He jumped back on his horse and galloped off to the head of the procession. His spear-pointing samurai followed him.

The lady spoke to the girls and got back in her traveling box.

The three girls walked toward us. As they came closer we could see that they weren't Japanese. Something about them looked very familiar.

"Hi, Joe," said the girl who had spoken.

"Hi, Sam," said the girl with the crazy wild hairdo.

"Hey, Fred," said the girl wearing samurai pants like Honda's.

Just when we thought things couldn't get any stranger, Fred, Sam, and I said hello to our great-granddaughters.

Now I realize a sentence like that last one has probably never been written before. Most people don't get a chance to say hello to their great-granddaughters. It's a long and complicated story. I'll give you the short version.

In the past we went one hundred years into the future. We met our great-granddaughters— Jo, Samm, and Freddi. They inherited *The Book*. So they can travel anywhere in time, too. Don't ask me how or why or if it messes up the universe. I have no idea. We're always too busy saving ourselves to answer any questions. Check out our adventure called *2095* if you still think you need to know more.

The girls untied our hands. We tried to act like we knew what we were doing.

"Oh hey," I said.

"What's up?" said Fred.

"Ancient Japan," said Sam.

"Do you realize you were about to get speared for insulting a samurai?" said the crazy-hair girl, Samm. "I don't know what you said to Owattabutt, but he's the wrong guy to get mad at you."

"Oh what a butt," said Fred.

Sam and I laughed.

The girls gave us a blank look. I'm pretty sure I saw Jo roll her eyes.

"You should be more careful about flipping the Auto-Translator off and on," said Samm. "You had it off, you know."

"We know," said Sam. "We were just . . .uh . . . practicing counting to ten in Japanese."

"We're visiting our friends, Lady Ii Naomasa and Lady Ieyasu Tokugawa," said Jo, holding out her arms to show off her kimono. "Isn't seventeenth-century Japan amazing?"

"Yeah," I said. "Amazing anyone keeps their head on their shoulders for very long."

"You've got to check out the samurai training," said Freddi. "I wanted to come back to do some more work on my sword moves." She spun through a few moves with a wooden samurai practice sword.

I saw Honda nod. Zou smiled.

Jo noticed Honda and Zou. "Oh these must be the Time Guides you picked."

"Huh?" I said.

"No," Samm said to Jo. "They must be on total Auto Travel. *The Book* picks everything. I'll bet they don't even know where to find *The Book*."

Jo looked at us. She couldn't be too mean. She is my great-granddaughter. "So were you going to warp home through the poetry contest, or wait for the next Time-Space Fold?"

I remembered the haiku that got us here. "Poetry contest," I guessed.

"Well, let's get going," said Jo. "You can introduce us to your friends."

We had no idea what she was talking about, but we followed Jo, Samm, and Freddi. We introduced Honda and Zou.

We walked down the seventeenth-century Tokaido Road toward Edo and the samurai warlord Tokugawa's castle like we were strolling to the deli.

Time travel will do that to you.

# ELEVEN

It would take me a whole book to tell all of the strange stuff we saw and did next. It was like being on a different planet. In fact, it would probably take me two whole books. And I'm not that crazy about writing. So I thought I might make the next couple of pages like the part in movies where they show a lot of short scenes all mashed together. It's usually in those lame movies when people are supposed to be falling in love. Or in the action movies when the good guy is getting ready to fight the bad guy. Sam told me the name for that, but I forget what it is. But now that I think of it, it's kind of like haiku. Short and to the point.

* * *

Pine trees along the Tokaido road. Hills. Waterfront. Over a bridge and into the crazy busy city of Edo. Buildings of wood, paper windows. Looking

like New York in kimonos. Samm telling us, "Edo, as you know, is the original name of modern Tokyo." Sam says, "I knew that."

\* \* \*

At a roadside food stand. Fred eating noodles (*soba*). We all eat raw fish on rice (*sushi*) with our chopsticks (*hashi*). Seaweed, shrimp, hard-boiled eggs I recognize. Zou and Freddi eating octopus (*tako*).

* * *

The heart of the city. A great wide street full of shops and a sea of people. A bookshop. "Do you have a thin blue book?" asks Sam. Swordmaker sharpening a pair of swords on a long flat stone. Honda tests his blades. Candlemaker. Oil seller. Puppet plays on the street. Silk sellers. Clowning entertainers. A basket full of kites. Bamboo brooms sweeping.

* * *

People, people, people on the street. Big flat round hats. Slow, pale, kimono-wrapped ladies. Everyone steps aside for proud samurai. Shaved-head priests and nuns. Sandals. "Look at that guy's socks with a big toe," I say. "Everyone wears those," says Jo, showing me hers. "They're called *tabi*." I say, "I knew that."

* * *

No one pays much attention to us. The Red Devils are a much more impressive sight . . . and proud of it. Red Devil samurai and soldiers show off spears, lances, bows and arrows.

&#42; &#42; &#42;

Giant sweeping white stone wall. Passport check.
Lady Ii Naomasa guides us through. Bridge over
water-filled moat. A monster gate. Huge stone
walls of the castle rise up to little narrow windows,
just big enough to shoot an arrow through. Castle
samurai and soldiers with different armor, blue
banners.

&#42; &#42; &#42;

Inside paper walls, sliding doors. "You're asking
us to take a bath?" says Fred. "Sam, check that
Auto-Translator." Fred, Sam, and I soak in a giant
warm bath. A lady tries to talk us into kimonos.
Fred, Sam, and I get safely back in our jeans,
T-shirts, and sneakers. Jo, Samm, and Freddi in
even wilder outfits than before—patterned kimonos, wide belt things. Something is going on
with their hair.

&#42; &#42; &#42;

Honda: "Bushido is the Way of the Warrior."
    Fred and Freddi practice with wooden samurai
swords.
    The seven martial arts.

70

"Fencing." Whack.

"Archery." Whack.

"Spearmanship." Whack.

"Jujutsu." Whack.

"Horsemanship." Whack.

"Firearms." Whack.

"Military strategy." Whack.

"And girls trained as samurai, too," says Freddi. Fred blocks the last blow. "I knew that."

* * *

Sam and Samm sit cross-legged, listening to Zou. "The true samurai is a trained warrior, a trained artist, a trained mind," says Zou.

Carefully pouring tea into small cups. Samm arranges a stalk of flowers. Sam meditates in a garden of carefully raked stones.

A long thin flag over the castle flaps in the wind.

"What is moving?" asks Zou.

"The flag is moving," says Sam.

"The wind is moving," says Samm.

"Not the flag. Not the wind," says Zou. "Mind is moving."

* * *

Jo and I sit on our knees at a low table. "Samurai practice with swords . . . and brushes." Jo draws a neat Japanese character.

I draw. Try to act casual. Find *The Book*. Ask, "So you were thinking of warping home with haiku, too?"

Another neat character by Jo. "*Haikai*, actually. It's a whole chain of verses. Modern haiku came from that. The verses linked all together are called *renga*."

I draw. "Right," I say. "I knew . . . it was something like that. Five syllables, seven syllables, five syllables?"

Jo draws another perfect-looking character. "Oh no, that's just a simplification for English speakers. It's more about images. Like the famous poem of Basho:

> "Old pond . . .
> A frog leaps in
> Water's sound."

"Ms. Basho, our teacher?" I say.

"No, Basho the famous poet who will be born in 1644," says Jo. "Let me see your calligraphy."

I hold up my lettering. It's a nice graffiti: JOE

\* \* \*

Fred, Sam, and I kneel facing Freddi, Samm, and Jo.

"Wow," says Sam. "What a day. If this were a movie it would be a great montage."

"Yeah, that was the word I was looking for," I say. "So about *The Book*—"

A castle samurai slides open the screen wall behind us.

"Lord Tokugawa will see you now."

"Okay," says Sam. "We'll be right there. We just have to figure out—"

"*Now*," says the samurai.

We believe he means it.

# TWELVE

There was something very scary about being called before Tokugawa—the guy we knew would soon become the samurai shogun of all Japan.

Maybe it was the twelve fully armed, folded-ponytail, fancy-dressed samurai. Six knelt in a row on either side of us.

Maybe it was the ladies with their eyebrows shaved off and repainted higher on their foreheads.

Maybe it was the quiet and everyone looking at the six of us kneeling down in front of Tokugawa's raised platform.

I think it was mostly us knowing Tokugawa could do whatever he liked with us. That and the fact that I still didn't have the foggiest idea how this whole haiku, *renga, Book* time warping thing was supposed to work.

On the way in I saw Honda and Zou at the very

back of the long room. They were the only friendly faces I saw. I did see Owattabutt. He was not a friendly face.

We knelt there silently for what seemed like hours. You would have been proud of us. We acted very serious and didn't say a word. Finally someone broke the silence.

"Young strangers," said Tokugawa. "I have heard many thoughts from others, telling me who you are. Now I would like to hear from you."

We all looked up from our kneeling bows. Tokugawa sat above everyone wearing a huge wide-shouldered  kimono. Did he have two samurai swords? Is my name Joe? Tokugawa looked every bit like the general of generals that he was.

So this is going to take the trick of all tricks, I thought. I took a deep breath, hoping the Auto-Translator was still in working order. "I am Joe. This is Fred, Freddi, Sam, Samantha, and Jo. We are travelers from a far-off time and place—Brooklyn."

"You see, Lord?" said Owattabutt. "Outsiders, just as I said." Samm was right about making that guy an enemy.

Tokugawa held up his hand for silence. He turned to the lady just behind him. It was Jo, Samm, and Freddi's friend. "Lady Tokugawa?"

"Yes, Lord Tokugawa, they are outsiders. But students of our arts and way of life."

"Sorcerers, more likely," said Owattabutt. "That one turned a poor old woman into a bird. I questioned people who saw it. At the very least, they are enemy spies."

Tokugawa turned his fierce gaze on us. "So you see my problem. Students? Sorcerers? Spies?"

I had a sinking feeling there was no trick that could answer that question.

"That's it," said Fred. "Let's dive through that paper wall and get out of here before they toss us in the dungeon . . . or worse."

"I don't want to lose my head," said Sam. "I like my head."

Jo whispered, just loud enough for us to hear, "Time to go."

Then she spoke so everyone could hear.

"I think I can answer that question, Lord

78

Tokugawa. If I may ask the priest Zou to bring us our book of poems, we will answer in the form of a *renga* for your entertainment."

Lord Tokugawa's face changed from frowning general to kid in a candy store. "*Renga*? You are outsiders but know *renga*? Delightful. Please do."

Lady Tokugawa gave a little smile. Owattabutt ground his teeth loud enough for us to hear.

"A what-ga?" asked Fred.

"This isn't a dance, is it?" said Sam.

"I hope you know what you are doing," I said.

Jo smiled at us. Samm frowned. Freddi looked like she would have whacked me with a sword if she had one.

Zou handed Jo her "book of poems." I looked at the book and could have kissed him and her, I was so happy. The "book of poems" was a thin, blue, silver-writing, thank-goodness, time warping *Book*.

Jo thanked Zou with a bow. She turned to us. "That was fun. Maybe we'll see you some other time."

"But quit messing around with the Auto-Translator," said Samm. "It really wears on the Probability Mechanism."

79

"The what?" said Fred.

"We will," said Sam. "But what the heck is a *renga*, and how do we do one?"

"Short verses linked together," said Jo. "Each one connects with the verse before it. The whole thing tells a story by hopping around. But the good news is, *The Book* scans your recent time memory, then writes out the verse you are thinking. All you have to do is read it."

"We knew that," said Fred, Sam, and I.

"Right," said Jo. "I'll start." Jo turned and knelt with *The Book* in her lap. She opened it and read:

> "Green morning mist
> A good day to travel."

She handed *The Book* to me. I thought about our day and saw my verse write itself. I read it out:

> "Red Devils
> Red ants
> Marching on the Tokaido Road."

Freddi read:

> "Wooden sword
> hack attack.
> Watch out, Great-granddad."

Fred read:

> "Hot steaming
> Noodles are
> Delicious."

Samm read:

> "A butterfly flaps its wings
> in Brooklyn.
> Storm in Edo."

Sam looked around the room of samurai, then at Zou. Without even reading, he spoke his verse:

> "Flag moving, wind moving
> Time warping
> Mind moving."

Tokugawa smiled a huge samurai smile.

The most peaceful swirl of green mist we have ever felt wrapped us up like a baby in its mom's arms. Time Warp poetry.

Zou and Honda dipped a slight farewell bow.

Fred, Sam, and I bowed to Freddi, Samm, and Jo. I had a feeling we probably would see them like Jo said, "some other time."

Then we disappeared like Mount Fuji behind the mist.

# THIRTEEN

The green mist drained away. Fred and I were back at Sam's kitchen table. Sam was back standing in his ready karate pose. The last of the mist slipped into *The Book*. Sam collapsed into a kitchen chair.

"Oh table. Oh books. Oh home," said Sam. He laid his hands on the table to make sure it was real. "It's so good to be home safe and sound."

Fred and I looked at him.

"Well, mostly sound anyway," I said.

"Safe," said Fred. "Definitely safe."

We kept looking at Sam, not quite knowing how to tell him.

"What?" said Sam. "What are you two staring at? That was a pretty amazing zen samurai verse I came up with, wasn't it?"

"Yeah, amazing," I said.

"Yeah, a real samurai verse," said Fred.

We couldn't take our eyes off Sam's head.

"A real samurai," I said. "I'll bet that's what happened. Your verse was so samurai, that *The Book*—"

The downstairs doorbell buzzer buzzed.

Sam jumped up. "That's probably my mom. Put *The Book* away. We'll tell her we learned all this stuff studying samurai."

"Oh yeah," said Fred.

I heard Sam's mom's footsteps coming up the stairs. Sam went to get the door.

Time warped and started speeding up.

There was no other way but to just tell him.

We couldn't take our eyes off Sam's head.

"Yeah, that's it," I said quickly. "We'll tell her we were studying samurai and got so carried away that you . . . uh . . . shaved half your head and put the rest of your hair in a ponytail."

Sam turned back and looked at Fred and me. He reached up to feel his samurai shave and ponytail.

"Sam Samurai," said Fred.

Time warped and ran out.

Sam's mom opened the door.

Ms. Basho                                    Joe
English Class                                Sam
Second Period                                Fred


### HAIKU, HOKKU


In our research for our haiku homework, we found out that haiku came from an earlier kind of poetry contest. Different poets wrote connected verses called renga. The first verse was called hokku. That's where haiku came from. So we decided to hook our homework together and write a renga and call it Time Warps.

Time Warps
by
Joe, Sam, and Fred


Swords, banners, armor
On Sam's kitchen table.
1600 Japan.

Samurai
In the shadows.
Don't lose your head.

Real samurai
Wear two swords.
Read comic books.

```
A smiling old woman
Flaps her wings.
Three girls land.

Hot steaming
Noodles
Are delicious.

Kimonos, castles,
Flag, wind,
Mind flapping

Half-shaved head
With ponytail.
Sam samurai.
```

Boys,
   You did come up with some interesting research on the origins of haiku. But you didn't follow the haiku form, and didn't each give three examples.

# C⁻

Ms. Basho